FOR BRYCE, DYLAN, JACOB, JENNA, AND JOSH
FIVE PEOPLE WHO MAKE ME HAPPY

Library of Congress Cataloging-in-Publication Data

Schwartz, Amy, author, illustrator.
100 things that make me happy / by Amy Schwartz.
pages cm
ISBN 978-1-4197-0518-2
[1. Stories in rhyme.] I. Title. II. Title: One hundred things that make me happy.
PZ8.3.S29744Aaf 2014
[E]—dc23
2013042633

Text and illustrations copyright © 2014 Amy Schwartz
Book design by Meagan Bennett

Printed and bound in China
10 9 8 7 6 5 4

For bulk discount inquiries, contact specialsales@abramsbooks.com.

ABRAMS
THE ART OF BOOKS SINCE 1949
115 West 18th Street
New York, NY 10011
www.abramsbooks.com

100 THINGS that make me HAPPY

by AMY SCHWARTZ

Abrams Appleseed
New York

RED SOCKS

BUILDING BLOCKS

LICKING THE
SPOON

THE **MAN** IN THE **MOON**

AN ORANGE HAT

AN ORANGE CAT

FUZZY **SWEATERS**

LONG **LETTERS**

SLIPPERY **FLOORS**

DINOSAURS

COMFY CHAIR

COUNTY FAIR

BABY **TOES**

A PUPPY'S **NOSE**

STICKY **GLUE**

THE CITY
ZOO

ZOOMING *PLANES*

CHUGGING **TRAINS**

BUCKET
TRUCKS

YELLOW DUCKS

GROCERY CARTS

FROSTED
HEARTS

GRANDMA'S
LAP

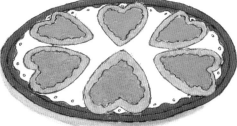

A GINGERSNAP

WHITE **SNOW**

COOKIE **DOUGH**

APPLE
PIES

BUTTERFLIES

LITTLE TRIKES

BRAIDS

PARADES

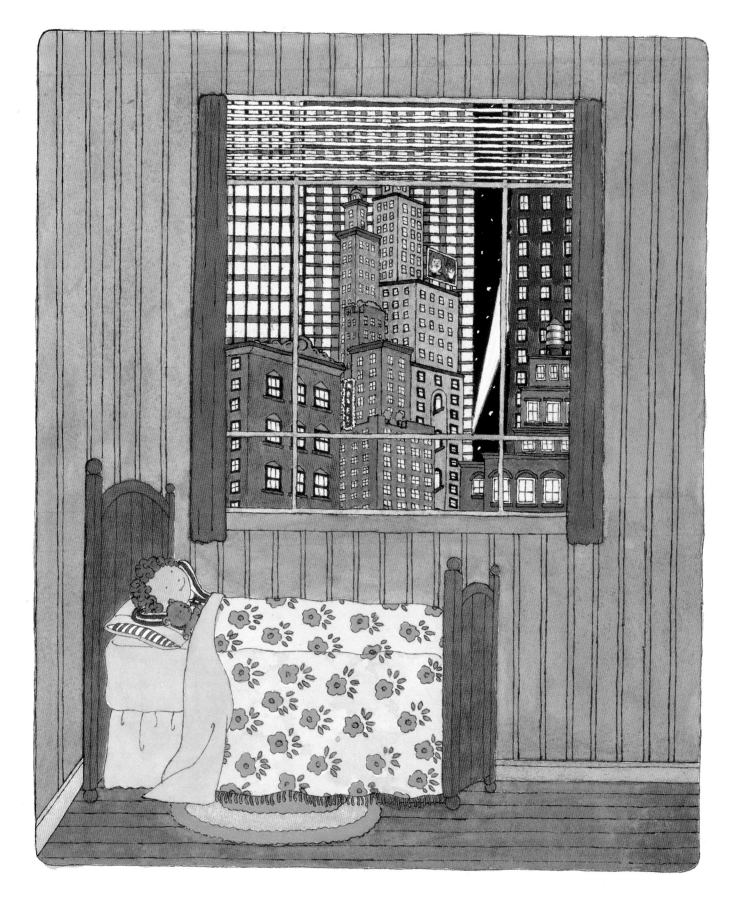

CITY LIGHTS

STARRY NIGHTS

POLKA **DOTS**

FORGET-ME-NOTS

PONY RIDES

SHINY SLIDES

SUBMARINES

JELLYBEANS

BIG **RIG**

GUINEA PIG

COZY **BED**

RAISIN **BREAD**

BUGS

HUGS

MITTENS

KITTENS

SNOWFLAKE

CHOCOLATE CAKE

CURLY **HAIR**

TEDDY **BEAR**

MERMAID

LEMONADE

CHOCOLATE **CHIPS**

CAMPING **TRIPS**

GOLDFISH

BIRTHDAY **WISH**

RED BOW

TIC-TAC-TOE

HULA-HOOPS

DOUBLE SCOOPS

THE **MILKY WAY**

SATURDAY

FLIP-FLOPS

LOLLIPOPS

FRENCH FRIES

FIREFLIES

DAYDREAM

WHIPPED
CREAM

ANYTHING
PINK

A WINK

SQUIRRELS

TWIRLS

TOYS

NOISE

SHOVELS
AND
PAILS

FAIRY TALES

STRAWBERRY ICE

PIZZA SLICE

BOUNCY **HOUSE**

WIND-UP **MOUSE**

HOME **RUN**

CINNAMON **BUN**

BEACH **BALL**

RAG **DOLL**

SOMETHING SWEET

PARAKEET

MUD **PUDDLES**

SOAP **BUBBLES**

GRANDPA'S **TOOLS**

SWIMMING **POOLS**

BROTHER AND SIS

GOOD-NIGHT KISS

HANDSTANDS

HOLDING
HANDS

GARBAGEMEN

A GOOD FRIEND

PEEKABOO

TIME WITH **YOU**!